Zee's Way

Kristin Butcher

D0802219

orca soundings

ORCA BOOK PUBLISHERS

Library and Archives Canada Cataloguing in Publication
Butcher, Kristin
Zee's way / Kristin Butcher.

(Orca soundings)
ISBN 978-1-55143-279-3

I. Title. II. Series.

PS8553.U6972Z43 2004 jC813'.54   C2004-900488-3

Summary: Zee is torn between making a statement with graffiti and making art.

First published in the United States, 2004
Library of Congress Control Number: 2004100594

Free teachers' guide available at: www.orcabook.com

Orca Book Publishers gratefully acknowledges the support for its publishing programs provided by the following agencies: the Government of Canada through the Book Publishing Industry Development Program and the Canada Council for the Arts, and the Province of British Columbia through the BC Arts Council and the Book Publishing Tax Credit.

The author gratefully acknowledges the financial support provided by the Canada Council for the Arts during the writing of this book.

Cover design by Lynn O'Rourke
Cover photography by GettyImages

In Canada: In the United States:
Orca Book Publishers   Orca Book Publishers
PO Box 5626, Station B   PO Box 468
Victoria, BC Canada   Custer, WA USA
V8R 6S4   98240-0468
www.orcabook.com
Printed and bound in Canada
on New Leaf Eco, 100% post consumer waste paper

11 10 09 08 • 7 6 5 4

For my grade seven teacher,
William Russell Donaldson,
who encouraged me to write.
—K.B.

Chapter One

I pushed open the bedroom window and stuck my head into the night. The rain had stopped right on schedule, and the clouds that had brought it were already scudding away. It had been like that all summer—hot sunny days, humid evenings and then—just after midnight—an hour of rain. Perfect conditions for a war.

Not that I wanted a war. None of the guys did. All we were after was a place to hang out. It was the merchants at Fairhaven Shopping Center who were looking for a fight.

As I stuffed the last of the cans into my pack, I thought back to the day Horace and I had visited the half-built mall. In an old neighborhood like ours, any kind of construction was worth checking out, but the guys and I had a real stake in this development. Before the dozers had come in and leveled everything, it had been our hangout. Maybe only an abandoned warehouse and parking lot to everybody else, but for us it was a place to chill. We could skateboard there, toss a baseball, kick a soccer ball or just get out of the rain.

At first we were super-ticked at being evicted, but after we got over the initial shock, we started thinking a shopping center might be just as good—even better if it meant an arcade or a fast-food joint. The thing is, we never got to find out. Two minutes after we stepped onto the site, some lunatic came after us with a crowbar.

For what? All we were doing was having a look around. Since when was that a crime?

"Don't get all bent out of shape about it," my dad said when I told him what had happened. "That shopping strip has been financed by the businesses moving into it. Those merchants are just protecting their investment."

I shook my head and walked away. I should have known my dad would take their side.

I zipped my backpack and slung it over my shoulder. Then I boosted myself onto the window ledge, swung my legs over the sill and dropped to the ground. Staying in the shadows, I peered at the old, shingled houses crowding the street. If any of the neighbors saw me taking a midnight stroll, my dad would know about it before breakfast. Then I'd have some explaining to do. But aside from the streetlamps, Barrett Avenue was dark. Mrs. Lironi's living room light was on, but that didn't mean she was up. She just kept the light on to discourage burglars. Everyone knew that—even the burglars.

I jogged across the yard and hurdled the hedge. My shadow stretched along the road beside me, bent arthritically where it climbed the curb. From the corner of my eye, I could see it matching my pace, and I was grateful for the company. I ran past a soggy flyer plastered to the sidewalk. It reminded me of the one the shopping center had put out for its grand opening.

That had been a huge event. Everyone in the neighborhood had come out for the bargains. Two for one at Oscar's Video Emporium, no GST at The Loonie Bin and 25 percent off all prescriptions at Fairhaven Drugs. Mario's Coffee Bar was selling large cappuccinos for the price of small ones, and there were free deli samples at Jackman's Market.

There was stuff going on in the parking lot too. Barbecues were sizzling up hot dogs and hamburgers. A clown with size thirty shoes was making balloon animals. Another one was painting faces. There was even a marching band. The local radio station was there too.

The guys and I showed up around one o'clock. By that time the place was so packed we could barely move. I squinted up at the white banner stretched across the storefronts. Fairhaven Shopping Center— Grand Opening! Something for Everyone, it said in huge blue letters.

But the second we arrived, the party was over. Oh, the festivities didn't stop; we just weren't allowed to be part of them.

It was discrimination, plain and simple. Not that the merchants came right out and told us to get lost. They just acted like we weren't there. Except when they thought we weren't looking. Then they couldn't stop staring.

Okay, so the five of us don't exactly blend into a crowd. Danny's got blue hair and Horace's head is shaved. Benny's lip is pierced, Mike has a thing for leather and studs, and we all have tattoos. So what! If our money's good, it shouldn't matter what we look like.

Try telling that to the Fairhaven merchants. Their minds were made up. They didn't want us around—not that first day or any day after that.

Whenever we'd go into a store, someone would follow us. Don't handle the merchandise. Don't read the magazines. Don't block the aisles. It was a song that played just for us. Women pushing strollers could jam the aisles. Old people could pick up the merchandise. Middle-aged men could browse the magazines. It was just fifteen-year-old guys who weren't allowed.

It was the same thing outside the stores. All we had to do was stand on the walkway in front of a shop and the owner would glare at us until we moved on. We couldn't even skateboard through the parking lot without getting yelled at. But since we had nowhere else to go, we put up with it.

Until the No Loitering signs went up. That's when we decided it was time to take a stand. Not that we really did anything different than what we were already doing.

We just did more of it. And we did it on purpose.

Except for breaking the window in Jackman's Market. That was a total accident.

It was a Sunday morning. The shopping center wasn't open yet, so we were using the parking lot as a soccer field. The problem was that Benny didn't know his own strength. Before any of us realized what had happened, he'd kicked the ball through Jackman's window and set off the alarm.

We didn't wait around for the police. Accident or not, we knew we'd be blamed. And we were right. The store owners said the soccer ball was all the proof they needed. From then on they treated us like criminals. We were only allowed in a store two at a time—and only for five minutes. When we came out, we had to clear off the property completely. If we stood around for even thirty seconds, a police cruiser would show up.

I looked at the sky. The clouds were completely gone now, and I could see the glow of the shopping center lights ahead.

On the corner of Madison and Harper, I pressed close to a big oak tree and peered up and down the deserted street. Then when I was sure the coast was clear, I bolted across the road.

Feniuk's Hardware was the last store on the strip. There was nothing between it and the sidewalk except a Dumpster. I ducked behind the Dumpster and gazed up at the wall of the store. Bathed in the light of a nearby streetlamp, it was embarrassingly white and empty.

I pulled one of the spray cans from my backpack and began shaking it. Then I looked at the wall again.

It wouldn't be empty for long.

Chapter Two

The reason I painted the wall at night was so no one would see me. But darkness—the thing that makes night a good time for hiding—also makes it a crummy time for painting. Darkness blurs lines and erases details. And it sucks the life out of spray paint until every color looks gray.

So when I returned to the scene of the crime the next morning, it was like I was seeing that graffiti for the first time. I had no sooner stepped onto Madison Boulevard than the three-foot-high words started screaming at me!

My first impulse was to hurl myself at the wall and smother them into silence. My second impulse was to make a run for it. But I didn't do either of those things.

Instead, I went and stood beside Horace, who was leaning against the oak tree.

He wagged a thumb at the wall and the stunned shopkeepers huddled in front of it. "You did that?" There was surprise in his voice.

"Yeah. So?" I muttered defensively. Last night the graffiti had seemed like a good idea, but now I wasn't so sure.

Horace's big face broke into a grin. He shrugged. "I'm just surprised, that's all. I mean, it's not like the paintings you usually do, is it?"

"That's because it's *not* a painting," I corrected him. "It's *graffiti*." I didn't want anybody confusing what was on the wall with real art.

Horace shrugged. "Graffiti, painting—it's all the same to me." Then he gave me a hip check that moved me over a couple of feet.

"Hey!" I protested.

Horace flexed his arm and admired the barbwire tattoo circling his bicep. "Sorry, man. Sometimes I forget my own strength."

I couldn't argue with that. Horace was built like a small mountain, and even his good-natured nudging tended to leave bruises.

"How come you didn't let me in on the plan?" he asked.

"Because I didn't have a plan," I said. "The idea just sort of came to me when I found the spray paint in my basement."

Horace nodded and pointed toward the shopping center. "Looks like things are heating up over there. If the old lady from the flower shop waves her arms any faster she's gonna go up like a helicopter." He laughed at his own joke and then shouted across the street, "Nice paint job! Who's your decorator?"

The merchants swiveled toward the sound, their curiosity turning to anger as soon as they saw us. Then the owner of Jackman's Market began stomping toward the road. Horace and I kept leaning against the tree. *Be cool*, I told myself as the muscles in my legs tensed for takeoff.

One of the other merchants grabbed Jackman's arm. "Forget it, Leo," he said. "They're just trying to get your goat. Don't give them the satisfaction."

Jackman stopped. He glowered at us. Then he shook his fist. "Punks!" he yelled. "That's what you are—punks! Sneaky, good-for-nothing punks!" He waved his arm at the wall. "Look at this mess! You've got no right defacing people's property like that."

"And you got no right accusing people of a crime without any proof!" Horace yelled back.

Technically, he was right. The merchants didn't have any proof, so they shouldn't assume we were the ones who'd done the graffiti. But the truth is, we *had* done it—well, I had anyway. Suddenly I felt like a criminal.

Jackman dismissed Horace's objection. "You haven't even got the guts to own up to what you did. Not that I'm surprised. Punks, I tell you. Somebody ought to take a belt to your backsides."

Horace sauntered to the curb and leaned out over the pavement. "Oh yeah? Like who, for instance? *You*?" Then he snorted and strolled back to the tree.

It was a dare, and Jackman took it. Purple with rage, he charged onto the road.

Beeeeeeeeep!!

From out of nowhere a car came speeding toward him. Jackman's arms went up and then he spun away and fell.

I stopped breathing. Time stopped ticking. It felt like we were going to be caught in that second forever.

Then suddenly everything started moving again. The shopkeepers rushed onto the road, and Jackman struggled to his knees. He hadn't been hit.

But the incident had shaken the merchants up enough that they forgot about Horace and me and headed back to their stores.

"We win that round," Horace announced after they'd gone.

"Maybe," I replied, "but you know they're—"

A bunch of clatters and clangs cut me off. Feniuk, the old guy from the hardware store, was trying to get a metal ladder out of his shop. It took a while, but he eventually won, leaned the ladder against the graffitied wall and went inside again. A minute later he was back, juggling rags, a paint can, a paint tray, brushes and a couple of rollers.

Horace patted me on the shoulder. "Too bad, Zee. It looks like your billboard is history."

While Feniuk painted over the graffiti, Horace and I sat in the shade of the oak tree and razzed him. Actually, Horace did the razzing.

"You missed a spot," he'd holler every

once in a while, or "Looks like it's gonna take a couple of coats," and sometimes, "You need a hand?" And then he'd clap.

As for me, I just watched. Heckling isn't really my style. Actually, graffiti isn't my style either. So it was almost a relief to see the fluorescent insults vanishing from the wall.

At the same time, though, it was also deflating. The graffiti had been a way of telling the merchants they were being unfair. And as each word was painted over, it felt more and more like they hadn't heard me. So why had I bothered?

After nearly two hours, Feniuk looked like he was going to keel over. He was red in the face and drenched in sweat. I could hear him puffing clear across the street. Anybody could see he was too old and out of shape for that kind of work—especially on such a hot day. So when he finally dragged the ladder back into his store, I was relieved. I had enough on my conscience without adding his heart attack to the list.

As soon as the door banged shut, Horace jumped to his feet. "What say we do a little shopping?"

"The graffiti may be gone," I pointed out, "but I don't think anybody's forgotten about it."

Horace shook his pants pockets. They jingled. "I got money, man, and I wanna spend some of it. We been sitting here all morning. I'm starved. Let's go to the market and get some donuts."

I couldn't believe my ears. "You got a death wish?" I said. "If we go in there, Jackman will kill us!"

Horace screwed up his face. "You think?"

"Obviously more than you."

"Maybe you're right." Then Horace's expression cleared again. "We can go see Jackman tomorrow." He headed for the road. "Come on."

"Come on where?" I asked suspiciously.

He turned and looked at me as if I was brain-dead. "I told ya, man. I'm starved. I need to eat. Let's go to the drugstore and get some chips or somethin'."

Reluctantly I got to my feet and started to follow him.

"Then we'll go to Feniuk's Hardware." Before I had a chance to protest, he jerked a thumb toward the wall, which was once again spotlessly white. "You're gonna need more paint."

Chapter Three

It seemed to me that going into the hardware store was like poking your nose into a hornets' nest after you've stirred up the hornets. Only an idiot would do it. Or—in the case of Horace and me—two idiots.

For the first few minutes all we did was wander the aisles. After that, we went to the paint department. Even though I'd told Horace I wasn't going to do any more graffiti, he piled spray paint cans into my arms. Then we headed for the checkout.

Feniuk was working the cash register. As soon as I saw him, I wanted to drop the paint and run. But if I did, I knew Horace and the other guys would never let me hear the end of it.

So I plunked the paint onto the counter and waited for whatever it was Feniuk was going to do. He looked at the cans; then he looked at me. I knew he knew what the paint was for. The question was, what was he going to do about it.

To my surprise, he didn't do anything. He just rang in the sale and told us to have a nice day.

I was stunned. Our little visit hadn't gone anything like I'd thought it was going to. Not only had Horace and I made it out of the hardware store alive, we'd been told to have a nice day! Did that mean the merchants were ready to call a truce?

On that hope, I took the spray paint home and stashed it under my bed.

A week later I hauled it out again.

Instead of getting better, things had gotten worse. Jackman had banned Horace and me from his store completely. And he wasn't kidding around. He even threatened to fire any staff that let us in. It's a wonder he hadn't slapped up Wanted posters.

But since Danny, Mike and Benny were still allowed in the market, they bugged Jackman for us. As Mike went out one door, Benny went in another. When he left, Danny showed up. Mostly the guys just kept the clerks chasing them around the store—though they did manage to add a frog to the lettuce display and swipe the pricing signs in the canned goods aisle.

We knew the fun couldn't last though. In fact, it only took one day for Jackman to kick the other guys out of his store too. So they egged his windows. That's when the cops started patrolling the shopping center on an hourly basis, and since we were what they were looking for, we stayed away.

"Loser!" Mike shook his fist at Jackman's Market from the safety of the oak tree. "You're a freakin' moron, Jackman! We got rights, you know!"

"What gave you that idea?" Horace said sarcastically.

"You know what I mean," Mike scowled, smacking the studs of his leather wristband against the tree.

"Mike's right," Danny said. "We're being persecuted! And it's not fair. It's not right. It's against the law!"

Horace frowned. "Well, there's no use cryin' about it. We need to do something." Then he nodded toward the street.

We all turned just as a police car drove past real slow. The cops inside looked us over but kept driving. We glared back. That's all. We didn't want them to stop.

After the cruiser turned the corner, Horace pushed himself away from the tree. "The way I see it, we got two choices. We can try to find someplace else to hang out—"

"There is no place else," Benny cut in.

Horace frowned. "I wasn't finished."

"Sorry," Benny apologized.

"As I was saying—we can find someplace else to hang out, or—" Horace paused, and when he started talking again he was smiling, "—*or* we can convince the store owners to change their minds."

In other words, we could step up the war. Until the merchants agreed to let us into their stores and treat us like human beings, we were going to do everything we could to make their lives miserable.

That's why I dug the spray paint out from under my bed. I still wasn't thrilled about painting the wall, but what could I do? The guys were counting on me.

On my first graffiti expedition, I'd had surprise on my side. But that wasn't the case anymore. For all I knew, the merchants were waiting for me to strike again. Come to think of it, maybe that's why Old Man Feniuk had sold me the paint. I could be walking into a trap!

I took a couple of deep breaths. There was no sense getting paranoid. But with cop cars crawling all over the place, I'd have to be extra careful.

Knock, knock, knock.

My stomach jumped. It still hadn't landed when the bedroom door opened, and my dad walked in. I'd been about to stuff the last two cans of spray paint into my backpack, but I quickly changed my mind and set them on the drawing table instead. With a little luck my dad wouldn't notice.

"Thanks for the privacy," I complained.

My dad looked offended. "What are you talking about? I knocked."

I glared at him. "What's the point if you walk in right after? I could've been naked or something."

He started to snicker. For some reason he found that funny.

I didn't.

"What do you want?" I growled.

His smile turned to a frown. "What is it with you? You're always so damn defensive.

I came to tell you I picked up a shift tonight. Wilcox is sick, so I'm taking his route. You'll be on your own. If you have to get hold of me, call the dispatch. The number's by the phone."

I nodded. I knew the drill. It wasn't the first time my dad had worked nights. He had a regular bus route during the day, but he was always willing to take on another shift. Especially since Mom left.

"What are your plans?" he said.

I shrugged. "Dunno. I don't really have any. Maybe I'll do some painting."

That was the truth, more or less, but the second the words left my mouth, I knew they were a mistake. My dad glanced at the drawing table and saw the spray cans. His eyes narrowed.

"What're you going to do with those?"

"These?" I picked up one of the cans. "I'm trying a new technique I saw in an art book. It's kind of like airbrushing, but you do it with spray paint." I figured that was a pretty safe answer since my dad knows absolutely nothing about art.

"Oh yeah?" he said. "The only thing I've ever seen spray paint used for is graffiti."

It felt like someone had broken my knees. Did my father suspect what I was going to do? I looked away to hide my guilt.

But he was too wrapped up in his own thoughts to notice. "That damn stuff is everywhere," he began to rant. "Park benches, tunnels, Dumpsters, overpasses, even mailboxes! I see it all day long. It's a bloody eyesore! As fast as you paint over it, it's back again. You can't even tell what it's supposed to say. Obviously it doesn't take a whole lot of brains or talent." He threw up his hands. "You had to get me started, didn't you!" Then, muttering under his breath, he stormed off down the hall.

Chapter Four

That's how most conversations with my dad go—one of us ends up yelling and walking away. And no matter who it is, I'm always left feeling like someone dumped a beaker of acid in my gut.

This time the thing that set my stomach churning was the crack about graffiti artists having no talent or brains. If my dad felt that way, it was a safe bet other people did too. And though I knew that shouldn't matter, it did. I didn't want anyone thinking I was stupid.

I picked the paintbrushes up off the table. I didn't want them thinking I had no talent, either.

The next morning the guys gathered around the oak tree to check out my work.

"That's way cool, man!" Benny grinned at me and then at the wall of Feniuk's Hardware.

"No kidding!" Danny agreed. "It looks like a real door. I bet if we keep watching, someone will try to open it."

Everybody laughed.

I didn't say anything, but inside I was smiling. The door I'd painted on the wall did look almost real—from across the street anyway. It was the right height, it had a jamb and a sill, and the glass in the window looked like it was reflecting sunlight. I'd like to hear my dad say that didn't take talent.

But, of course, he was never going to see it. Today was his day off, and after working a double shift, he wouldn't be out of bed until sometime in the afternoon. By then it would be too late. The door would be gone.

As if on cue, Feniuk banged his way out of the hardware store with his painting supplies. One of his employees trailed behind with the ladder. You could tell the guy was volunteering to do the painting, but Feniuk waved him away.

When the clerk had gone back inside, the old man stared at the wall for a couple of minutes. I guess he was trying to figure out where to begin because—except for the door—it was one big tangle of graffiti.

He finally headed for the end farthest from the Dumpster and started painting. Little by little the graffiti disappeared as he worked his way toward the middle. When he got to the door, he moved to the other end of the wall and began painting his way back again. Then, pulling a handkerchief out of his pocket, he wiped the sweat from his forehead and stepped back to look at his work.

The only thing left to do was the door.

As Feniuk loaded the roller with paint, I felt my body stiffen. I glanced down at my hands. They were fists. I unclenched them, but ten seconds later they were tight balls again.

Feniuk was going to paint the door. It wasn't like I hadn't known it was going to happen. So why was I letting it bug me?

Because that door was art—maybe not a Rembrandt or a van Gogh, but it was still art. *My art*—and I didn't want it destroyed. I tried to look away, but I couldn't do that either.

Feniuk raised the roller to the top of the door and touched up a spot on the concrete block just above it. Then he walked the length of the wall, looking for other places he'd missed. Finally he returned to the door, picked up his paint supplies and headed into the hardware store. A couple of minutes later the clerk came out to collect the ladder.

Instantly Horace and the other guys started whooping and hollering and giving each other high fives. They seemed to think we'd scored some kind of major victory.

Maybe we had, but that wasn't how it felt to me.

I couldn't stop staring at the wall. The graffiti was gone, but the door was still there. Considering I hadn't wanted it destroyed, I should have been relieved. But the truth is, I felt worse than ever.

And that's because I'd just been robbed. The door, the jamb, the sill, the reflected sunlight, even the Closed sign that I'd painted in the window—they were all still there, but they didn't belong to me anymore. Feniuk had stolen them. He'd painted over the graffiti because he didn't want it. But he'd kept the door. Why?

And how was I going to get it back?

The way I figured it, no one would expect me to paint graffiti two nights in a row. So that's exactly what I was going to do.

I got to the hardware store around 1 a.m. and immediately started pulling spray cans from my pack. They felt pretty light, but there'd been no time to get more paint. Anyway, if I'd tried to buy some, Feniuk might have gotten suspicious. I was just going to have to make do with what I had.

I worked fast, draining every drop from the cans. When the last one was dead, I chucked it into the Dumpster and headed for the door. Digging a charcoal stick out of my pack, I sketched in the changes I wanted. Then I cocked my head to one side and squinted, trying to visualize the way it would look when it was finished.

Dumping brushes and tubes of acrylic onto the pavement, I got right to work. It was just a matter of painting some new things over some old ones. I'd already planned it out, so it came together pretty quickly. Closed sign gone, replaced by a big hole in the window. Glass shards lying on the ground nearby. Soccer ball sitting beside them.

I took a step back to study the finished product. Perfect! It said everything. The way the door looked now, there was no way Feniuk would leave it on his wall. He'd be out with his roller as soon as the sun came up. That was what I wanted, but at the same time it was a depressing thought. I stared at the door some more, trying to paint it into my memory in case I never saw it again.

From the corner of my eye I caught the glare of headlights at the other end of the block. I dove behind the Dumpster. Then I looked back toward the wall. My pack and all my supplies were still sitting in the middle of the sidewalk, plain as day, but I didn't dare go back for them. I held my breath and waited.

Then the lights passed by and the car was gone.

But I'd gotten the message. It was time to beat it out of there.

I scrambled back to the sidewalk and started cramming everything into my pack. At least I tried to. But nothing wanted to go. Paint tubes squirted through my fingers; brushes got caught in the sidewalk cracks. My water bottle rolled away.

"Damn!" I swore, making a grab for it.

And that's when I realized there was someone standing near the end of the wall. I looked up. My mouth went dry. It was a man with a baseball bat.

"I thought I might find you here tonight," he said.

Chapter Five

My feet were moving before my hands could even grab the backpack. As for my brain—it wasn't working at all. My heart was pumping straight adrenaline, and all systems had switched to automatic pilot. I had one goal—get away from Feniuk as fast as I could. In a matter of seconds I'd put the Dumpster between us and was halfway across the boulevard. I glanced over my shoulder. The old man hadn't moved.

I felt my body start to relax. This was no contest. Feniuk was old and out of shape. Even if he tried, he wouldn't be able to keep up the chase for more than half a block. And though he had a baseball bat, it wasn't much of a threat if he couldn't get close enough to use it.

With that thought in mind, I turned on the jets and tore onto the road. In another minute Feniuk wouldn't even see me, let alone catch me.

"John Zeelander."

My brain didn't believe my ears, but my feet did. They froze in mid-stride and I went sprawling. But just as fast, I was up and moving again.

"John Zeelander!" Feniuk called once more, louder this time.

I hesitated. *He knew my name*!

"423 Barrett Avenue." Feniuk struck again before I could gather my wits.

I could feel the blood draining from my face, and though the night was warm, my skin turned to gooseflesh. *Feniuk knew my address too*!

"844-9736."

And my phone number!

That's when reality set in and I stopped running. It didn't matter how much distance I put between Feniuk and me, I wasn't going to get away from him.

So I just stood in the middle of the street, waiting for the police cars to close in. The sirens, the flashing lights—I'd seen it in the movies a dozen times.

But this wasn't a movie. It was real life. There were no police cars. But that didn't change the fact that I was in more trouble than I'd ever been in before.

I tried to think what was going to happen next. Was Feniuk going to beat the hell out of me with that baseball bat? He didn't look like the violent type, but you could never tell. More than likely he'd turn me over to the police. Then I'd end up in juvenile court and probably jail. But before all that, the cops would call my dad.

I cringed at the prospect. I'd rather face the baseball bat.

Swinging it onto his shoulder, Feniuk began walking along the sidewalk. He took his time. Once he got past the Dumpster, he stopped and motioned to me.

"I think it's time we had a talk." The way he said it you'd have thought he was suggesting a chat about the weather.

I took a deep breath and started moving toward him. Whatever was going to happen, there was no point putting it off. I got as far as the boulevard. Then I stopped.

I guess Feniuk must've seen me eying the bat, because he took it down from his shoulder and leaned it against the wall.

He shrugged. "Protection. Can't be too careful. I'm not as young as I used to be." He squinted at the fresh graffiti. "Which is why I'm not enjoying this little game as much as you apparently are."

"It's not a game," I snarled. No sense letting him see I was scared. He had enough advantage as it was.

Feniuk must've heard the attitude in my voice. He looked at the bat like maybe putting it down hadn't been such a good idea. But he didn't pick it up again, and after a couple of seconds he walked away. Dumb move. Another kid would've grabbed that bat and clobbered him with it. I resented the fact that he didn't think I would.

"How do you know my name?" I growled.

He glanced over his shoulder. "I didn't hire a private detective, if that's what you're thinking. You and your friends are pretty well-known around here. So I asked a few questions, got out the telephone book and there you were."

As easy as that! Now, on top of being scared and mad, I also felt stupid.

"So what are you going to do?" I glowered at him.

"Me?" He shook his head. "I'm not going to do anything. You, on the other hand, are going to do quite a bit."

I folded my arms belligerently over my chest. "You can't make me do anything."

He nodded. "You're right. And that's why I'm not going to try. I'm an old man. You think I don't know that?"

I didn't say anything. I just kept glaring at him. We both knew he had an ace up his sleeve, and sooner or later he was going to play it.

He kept walking until he reached the center of the wall. Then he turned to face it. For the longest time he studied the changes I'd made to the door. "Uh-huh, uh-huh," he muttered over and over, but that was all.

Finally he clasped his hands behind his back and—still staring at the wall and rocking on his heels— said, "I have a proposition for you."

A proposition? I hadn't been expecting anything like that. "What kind of proposition?" I said warily.

"Well, the way I see it, you have vandalized the wall of my store with your graffiti three times now. Twice I've painted over it, and as you can see—" he held out his arms to take in the wall, "it needs to be painted again."

He paused. Maybe he was waiting for me to say something, but I didn't.

He carried on. "You don't strike me as a stupid fellow, so I'm sure you can appreciate that paint costs money. The time it takes for me to put it on the wall is money lost too. Somebody has to be accountable for all that money. And from where I'm standing, that somebody is you."

"Are you saying you want me to pay you back for your labor and paint?" I tried not to let him see my relief, but the truth is I felt as if someone had just thrown me a life preserver. I had money in my savings account. I'd gladly fork over some of it if it would get me off the hook.

But as soon as Feniuk answered, I realized it wasn't going to be that easy. "Yes—and no," he said. "I have tallied the costs, and I've come up with what I think is a fair figure. What I propose is that you work off the debt."

"What!" I blurted. "Work it off? How?"

"The same way you accrued it." He glanced at the wall again. "You paint. I shall pay you a minimum hourly wage until your debt is repaid. You can start by covering tonight's graffiti. After that," he pointed to the door I'd made, "you can finish this."

"It is finished," I snapped.

He looked at the door some more and then at me. "Are you sure? It seems to me it still needs something."

I felt my back stiffen. "Well, you're wrong." No old man was going to tell me how to do my art.

He shrugged. "Suit yourself. If you don't like my proposition, we'll just have to settle the matter some other way. Should I call the police or your home?"

Chapter Six

By the time I crawled back through my bed-room window, there wasn't a whole lot of night left. I'd been up for nearly twenty hours, so I should have been exhausted. Maybe I was. But there was so much going on in my head, I didn't even consider sleeping.

I just threw myself onto the bed—clothes and all—and tried to think of a way out of the jam I was in.

But there wasn't a way out. It was a maze with no exit. No matter which way I turned, I was trapped. If I didn't paint the wall, Feniuk would tell my dad. If I did paint the wall, somebody else would tell my dad. The whole neighborhood shopped at Fairhaven. Someone was bound to see me there. Either way, I was dead.

Not literally, of course. In my whole life, my dad has only cuffed me a couple of times. He's a yeller, not a hitter. So why was I worrying? That was another thing I couldn't figure out.

I'm not sure when the darkness started leaking out of the night, but by the time my dad's alarm went off, the sun had taken over my room.

I listened to the familiar morning sounds—water running, electric razor buzzing, dresser drawers scraping open and then footsteps in the hall. I stared at the door, waiting for my father to come crashing through it, hollering his head off.

Of course it didn't happen—he couldn't

possibly know yet what I'd done—but that didn't stop me from imagining his reaction. And it didn't stop me from feeling relieved when his footsteps continued on to the kitchen.

I looked at the clock. Feniuk had told me to be at the hardware store by eight, and it was already after seven. But until I smelled coffee brewing, I stayed right where I was. There was no way I wanted to face my dad before he'd had his morning fix of caffeine.

He was well into his second cup by the time I got to the kitchen. He looked up from a flyer he was flipping through. Then he glanced at his watch and frowned.

"Are you sleepwalking or what?" he said. "It's not even 7:30. And it's summer break. Since when do you roll out of bed before noon?"

I took a huge swig of orange juice before answering. Lack of sleep had turned my arms and legs into deadweights, and I was hoping a little sugar would energize me. I wiped my mouth with the back of my hand and belched. "Look who's talking," I said. "Yesterday you slept until the middle of the afternoon."

"After I'd pulled an all-nighter, pal," he sneered.

Hadn't I just done the same thing? I shook my head and gulped down some more juice.

"See this?" Dad pointed to the flyer on the table. "It's a thirty-five inch television selling for half price. That's a great deal. We're talking two-tuner picture in picture, stereo sound, three line digital comb filter, multifunction timer, front A/V input jacks…"

I peered over his shoulder as he read out the TV's features. "Sounds good," I said when he finally stopped for a breath. "You should get it."

He squinted at me as if trying to decide whether or not I was serious. And then he grinned. A rare flicker of excitement lit up his eyes. "You know," he said, "maybe I will. A deal like this doesn't come along every day. And God knows we're due for a new TV. The old one is on its last legs. There's no telling when it's going to pack it in."

I nodded. "Could happen right in the middle of the Stanley Cup." Hockey is my dad's favorite thing, and missing a big game would probably kill him.

The mere thought made him wince. "Wouldn't that be a kick in the head!"

I dropped a couple of bread slices into the toaster. "Right. So why take the chance? Buy the TV."

As soon as I said that, my dad did an about-face and started arguing against the idea.

"I don't know. Maybe I'm rushing things. Half price is still a lot of money. And besides, where would we put a television that size? There's no way we could squeeze it in where the other one is."

Obviously Dad had flipped into his negative mode. It happened every time he got close to feeling good.

"So put it someplace else," I said, barely able to keep the irritation out of my voice.

"Like where?"

I poked my head into the living room and looked around. It was gloomy and messy. I tried to remember a time when the room had looked different, a time when there'd been flowers on the tables and the windows had let the sunshine in—a time when my mother had been there. It seemed like forever ago.

Not that Dad and I were total slobs. We ran the dishwasher and did the laundry. The Spotlessly White Cleaners did the rest. But their once-a-week visits couldn't stay ahead of the clutter, and mounds of junk had grown everywhere. My gaze came to rest on the chair and music stand in the far corner. Well, almost everywhere.

"Put the TV over by the window," I said, returning to the kitchen and plunging a knife into the peanut butter.

"No."

"Why not?" I knew I was treading on forbidden ground, but since I was already in a pot of trouble, what difference would a little more make?

"You know why not." Dad's voice was quiet, kind of like the calm before the storm. "That's your mother's place. It's where she writes her music and plays her cello."

I ignored the warning. "You're wrong."

Dad's head shot up and his eyes flashed, but not even that could stop me. I was going to have my say.

"She used to do those things." I raised my voice to discourage any interruption he might be planning. "But in case you haven't noticed, she doesn't do them anymore—at least not here. And that's because she left. Remember? She skipped out, took a hike, jumped ship. It doesn't matter what you call it. The end result's the same. She's not here! And she's not coming back!"

Dad sprang out of his chair so fast the table lurched and coffee slopped onto the flyer.

"Yes, she is!" he roared, as if shouting could make it true. "She is coming back! She's just taking time out to follow her dream. But she'll be back. You'll see. She'll come home. And when she does, she's going to want her music corner."

"*Time out*?" I practically choked on the words. "You don't take time out from family, Dad! What's the matter with you? You talk like Mom's on some kind of vacation. Why can't you face the truth? She walked out on us!"

There are no words to describe the look that came over my father. All I know is that it scared the heck out of me. I thought he was going to hit me. Maybe he thought so too. Maybe that's why he pushed past and slammed out the front door.

Chapter Seven

When I got to the hardware store, the ladder and paint supplies were already outside. That was fine with me. The sooner I got to work, the sooner I'd be finished, and the less chance anyone would see me.

I figured Feniuk must be inside the building, so I headed for the entrance and pushed on the door. It wasn't locked, and as it swung open, a bell jingled. Feniuk was standing dead ahead. He frowned at his watch and then at me.

"You're late. When I say eight o'clock, I don't mean five minutes after. I was just about to pick up the phone."

I rolled my eyes. "We're talking a lousy five minutes. What's the big deal?"

"In business, Mr. Zeelander, five minutes is a very big deal. It can mean the difference between making a sale and losing one. You see that sign on the door? It says we're open from nine to nine. If a customer shows up at one minute after nine, the store should be open. If my employees are late, it won't be, and the customer will go somewhere else."

I scowled. "I'm not your employee."

"Until your debt is paid, you work for me three hours every morning, Monday through Friday. That makes you my employee. Don't be late again." Then he turned away and started tidying the shelves.

I stared in disbelief. Feniuk was acting like he owned me.

As I opened my mouth to protest, he glanced over his shoulder.

"Time is wasting, Mr. Zeelander," he said quietly. "I suggest you get started."

The guys showed up just before the shopping center opened. Normally they'd still be sawing logs at nine in the morning, but there's no way they were going to pass up the chance to razz Feniuk while he painted over my latest graffiti. Except, of course, it wasn't Feniuk who was doing the painting.

"Zee? Is that you, man?" Horace yelled from the oak tree.

I checked to make sure Feniuk was nowhere around. Then I motioned for the guys to cross the road.

In a matter of seconds they were on me like a pack of wolves. "What are you doing? What's with the roller? Where's old man Feniuk? How come you're painting over the graffiti?"

I put my hands up for quiet. "Listen, would ya! He caught me."

"What are you talking about?"

"You heard me. Feniuk caught me. Last night, just as I was finishing the wall."

"What do ya mean, he caught you? Did he grab you or something?"

I shook my head. "No. But he had a baseball bat."

Danny's eyes opened wide. "Did he hit you with it?"

I shook my head again.

"So why didn't you run?" That was Benny.

Before I could explain, Feniuk came around the corner.

"Mr. Zeelander," he called from the end of the wall, "I hired you to paint, not talk."

Instantly Horace's mouth dropped open and he fell back a step. "What!" Then his face snarled up and he shoved me. "You're working for him?"

The other guys glared at me. They all thought I'd sold them out.

"It's not what you're thinking," I said. I needed to convince them that I wasn't a traitor. I pictured myself telling Feniuk exactly what to do with his paint roller. But I didn't dare say the words out loud. The old man would be on the phone to my dad before I'd finished the sentence. Then I'd have an even bigger problem. I'd just have to find another way to show the guys I hadn't gone over to the enemy. "I can't explain right now," I whispered so Feniuk wouldn't hear. "I'll tell you everything later. Meet me at my house at noon."

They didn't say a word. They just kept staring like they'd never seen me before.

"Mr. Zeelander!" Feniuk was getting impatient.

"Come on, guys. You gotta trust me." I hoped my voice didn't sound as desperate as I felt. "Once I explain, you'll see I didn't have a choice. I swear! Just be at my place at noon. Okay?"

As I waited for an answer, Feniuk began walking toward us. That was enough for Horace. He spat on the sidewalk and started back across the road. So, of course, the other guys followed him.

"Dissension among the ranks?" Feniuk said as he watched them go.

I had no idea what that meant, but I sure as heck wasn't going to ask. I sent Feniuk a dirty look and went back to slapping paint on the wall. Instead of going away, he stood there gabbing at me. The last thing I wanted was to get chummy with the person who was ruining my life, so I ignored him. Finally he got the hint and went back into the store.

I looked at my watch. I still had almost two hours to put in. I'd be lucky to stay awake that long, never mind push a roller. I was physically beat.

Unfortunately exhaustion hadn't reached my brain. It was still thinking about Horace and Benny and Danny and Mike. Feniuk had chased them away before they'd agreed to meet me. If I could talk to them, I was pretty sure I'd be able to make them see how Feniuk had trapped me. But if they wouldn't give me a chance to explain, there was nothing I could do.

The thought was depressing. It made me more tired than ever. I would have given anything to fall asleep and forget my problems. In less than twelve hours I'd managed to lose my friends, send my dad over the edge and get blackmailed by Feniuk. Could anything else go wrong?

It was a mistake even to think that.

As I was gathering up the paint supplies, I heard the flip-flop of thongs coming down Harper Street. I looked up just as the person wearing them rounded the corner onto Madison Boulevard.

It was Mrs. Polanski. She's the biggest busybody in town, and she lives right on my street. Quickly I looked away. If she saw me, she'd want to know what I was doing. And if she found out I was the one who'd been painting graffiti, it was guaranteed she'd tell my dad. I could feel her eyes burning holes in my T-shirt, but I didn't turn around. If I made like I didn't see her, maybe she'd go away. Right—and maybe my mom would be sitting in the living room when I got home.

The flip-flopping thongs picked up speed as Mrs. Polanski hurried across the road.

"Zee?"

Since she was right in my face, it was impossible to pretend I didn't hear her. So I acted surprised instead.

"Oh. Hi, Mrs. Polanski." Smiling really hurt. "Going shopping?" It was a long shot, but I was hoping I could sidetrack her.

No such luck.

"Never mind me," she frowned. "What about you? What are you doing here…?" Her voice trailed off as she glanced meaningfully at the paint things. Then her eyes narrowed and she started to wag her finger in my face. "Are you up to no good? Mrs. Ramsay said the storekeepers have been asking questions about you. You're not the one who's been writing terrible things all over this wall, are you?"

I opened my mouth to lie—what choice did I have?—but suddenly Feniuk was standing beside me. And he was beaming at Mrs. Polanski.

My stomach slid into my sneakers.

Chapter Eight

Though I don't know how to stop doing it, I've come to the conclusion that worrying is a waste of energy. What's going to happen is going to happen whether I worry about it or not. All worrying does is give me a head start at feeling awful. And sometimes it's for nothing.

Take Feniuk spilling the beans to Mrs. Polanski. I was a basket case thinking how my dad was going to freak out. But it didn't happen. And that's because Feniuk gave Mrs. Polanski the same story he'd given my friends—I was working for him. So there was nothing for my dad to freak out about.

As for how miserable life was going to be if my friends never spoke to me again, that didn't happen either. Horace and the boys were waiting at my house when I got there. And though they weren't very friendly at first, they warmed up after I told them how Feniuk had blackmailed me.

That night I slept like a log, and the next morning I woke up feeling great. I didn't even care that I had to report to Feniuk at the hardware store. I'd just put in my three hours and split.

Of course, it was going to be a bit more complicated than that, because now I had to paint the mural. And that meant coming up with an idea—preferably something that would make Feniuk sorry he'd ever forced me into doing it.

I dug around in my brain for inspiration. I could always plaster vines and flowers all over the wall. I was pretty sure Feniuk would hate that.

Yeah, but so would I. I went back to thinking.

My reason for doing graffiti in the first place was to show the Fairhaven merchants they were discriminating. So why not use the mural to send the same message? Good idea, but how was I supposed to do that? What could I paint?

Whatever it was, it had to start with the door. That was about the only thing Feniuk and I agreed on.

By the time I reached the hardware store, a glimmer of an idea had started to form in my mind. It was still pretty foggy—there were lots of details to work out—but at least I had a starting place.

I pushed open the front door at eight o'clock on the nose. Feniuk looked at his watch but didn't say anything. What could he say? I was right on time.

"I'm going to need a brush about an inch wide, a small can of brown or black paint—something quick-drying, like exterior latex—and some rags," I told him.

He looked surprised. "That's all?"

"For now—until I get everything sketched out."

His face cleared and he nodded. "Of course, of course. Are you going to need a ladder?"

I shrugged. "I guess so."

I hauled the ladder outside while Feniuk rounded up the supplies.

"There you go," he said, setting them on the sidewalk. Then he squinted toward the sun and flapped a hand in front of his face. "It's hot already. When that sun gets a little higher, it's going to be sweltering."

I didn't look up from the paint can I was opening.

"Where's your hat?" he asked. "You can't work in the sun without a hat. And sunglasses. You're going to need those too. The sun bouncing off that wall will blind you."

"I'll be fine," I muttered, moving the stepladder into position and climbing onto it. "I'm out in the sun every day and I never wear a hat. And I don't even own sunglasses."

"I have some in the store. You can use those," he offered.

"Look," I said, scowling down at him from my perch. "I told you I'm fine. So are you going to keep talking at me, or are you going to let me paint?"

Feniuk raised his hands in defeat. "Suit yourself. But if you change your mind…" He left the sentence hanging and went back into the store.

I took a deep breath and sized up the wall. It was big. This wasn't the first time I'd worked on it, of course, so I should have realized that. But when I was doing the graffiti, I wasn't thinking about the overall appearance. I was just scrawling words. If there were gaps between them or if they overlapped, I didn't care. It didn't matter what the finished product looked like.

But the mural was different. It was going to take a bit of planning to get everything in proportion.

I climbed down from the ladder and went over to the oak tree, where I had a view of the whole wall. For a good five minutes I just stood there and stared, trying to figure out the location of everything I wanted to paint. Then when I had an idea of sizes and shapes, I headed back across the street and started laying things out.

I thought about how hard it had been to paint in the dark. But that was nothing compared to working in the sunlight. The way the sun's rays ricocheted off the white wall, it felt like razor blades slashing at my eyes. I couldn't look without squinting, and after a while I couldn't look at all. Every time I tried, my eyes would water and I'd have to turn away.

Though it bugged me to admit it, Feniuk had been right about the sunglasses. And after an hour of fighting the glare, I finally swallowed my pride and asked to borrow his. I expected a big I-told-you-so or at least a smirk, but he just handed me the sunglasses and went back to what he was doing.

After that, the painting went better. The morning was really heating up, and I was sweating like crazy, but at least I could see what I was doing.

Around 10:15, Feniuk came to check on me.

"Here," he said, holding out a can of pop. Water droplets rolled down the sides and splashed onto the sidewalk. Suddenly I was dying of thirst.

"What's this?" I said.

"What does it look like?" Feniuk pushed the can into my hands. "It's a drink. Take it."

"Why are you giving it to me?" I asked suspiciously.

He shrugged. "The government has strict rules about working conditions for employees. You're entitled to a break." Then he turned around and headed back into the store.

By eleven o'clock I had the mural outlined on the wall—the basics anyway. It wouldn't seem like much to anyone else, but it was the skeleton I needed, and I was looking forward to starting the actual painting.

So when I headed into the hardware store to return Feniuk's sunglasses and wash out my paint things, I was feeling pretty good.

Until I overheard Mrs. Costello from the flower shop giving Feniuk a piece of her mind.

"You're a fool, Sam Feniuk," she was saying. "What you should be doing is calling the police. The boy is a hoodlum. Hasn't he proven that? He's going to rob you blind—or worse! Mark my words. Leo is right. Young people these days can't be trusted. Call the police before it's too late."

Chapter Nine

When I heard that, I felt like a race-car driver who's just bounced off a brick wall. I was totally stunned. And that's because during the last three hours—for the first time all summer—I hadn't been thinking about the war with Feniuk and the other merchants. That morning the only thing I'd had on my mind was the mural. I'd been so wrapped up in planning it out that I'd forgotten I was being forced to do it.

But Mrs. Costello's words jolted me back to reality. I wouldn't forget again.

"She really said that?" Benny's eyes widened with disbelief when I told the guys what I'd heard.

"Why are you so surprised?" Mike snorted. "We've known all along the storekeepers hate us."

"So let's give them a reason," Danny said.

"What kind of reason?" It was Benny again.

"Well, you know how Old Lady Costello puts buckets of flowers outside her shop during the day?"

We all nodded.

"What if we cut off all the tops so that only the stems are left?"

"Good one," Mike snickered.

"Better yet, why don't we just make a switch?" Horace suggested with a grin. "You know—weeds for flowers. You think people will pay $6.99 for a bunch of dandelions?"

We all laughed.

Then I got serious again. "But if we do any of that stuff, Feniuk might start thinking Mrs. Costello is right."

"Don't you think he already does?" Danny looked amazed.

I shrugged. "I guess, but he doesn't seem quite as determined to get us thrown in jail as Jackman and the others do. When he caught me doing the graffiti, he could've called the police, but he didn't. And he has kept his word about not telling my dad."

"So far," Mike replied skeptically. "But that could just be a trick. He might be sucking you in. Maybe he's waiting for you to finish the mural before he rats on you."

I shook my head. "I don't think so."

I had no idea why I was sticking up for Feniuk. I was as frustrated with the merchants as the other guys were. They'd done nothing but hassle us since the shopping center opened. It's just that I knew what it felt like to be judged unfairly, and I didn't want to do it to somebody else—not even Feniuk.

"I guess we'll just have to see what happens," Horace said. "Let Feniuk make the next move."

That was fine for Horace to say. He wasn't the one who'd have to answer to the cops and my dad if Feniuk did do something. But since I had no control over that, I just kept showing up at the hardware store and working on the mural.

By the third day, things were starting to come together. The mural was growing into a storefront. It didn't look like any of the stores in Fairhaven—no sense getting the merchants suspicious—but it still looked like a store.

Using a technique called trompe l'oeil, which literally tricks the eye into thinking a flat surface is three-dimensional, I painted a blue-and-yellow-striped awning the length of the wall. It looked so real it seemed to pop right out from the building. On each side of the door I put display windows. I drew a No Littering sign on the wall, and under it I placed a trashcan. On the ground beside that

I painted a candy wrapper, some crumpled paper and a discarded drink box. The end of the wall near the corner was the perfect spot for a big red mailbox. I even added some graffiti to it. At the other end—for balance—I put a fire hydrant, and just for laughs I included a dog sniffing it.

That's what I was working on when I suddenly got this feeling someone was watching me. I looked around.

Mrs. Costello was standing on the boulevard behind me. I had no idea how long she'd been there—or even how she got there without me noticing. But she was there. And after what she'd told Feniuk—young people can't be trusted—it gave me the creeps to have her watching my every move.

It was like she was waiting for me to screw up. I was tempted to paint the fire hydrant purple just to freak her out.

But I didn't. Even though it would have been fun to see her have a fit, I knew I could wait a few more days for that. Soon I'd be ready to put people into my mural, and that was bound to stir up a few of the merchants—including Mrs. Costello. I couldn't help wondering how she was going to like seeing herself on the wall. Just the thought of it made me smile.

From the corner of my eye I could see her walking along the boulevard. Every couple of feet she'd stop and study the mural. Then she'd move on again. When she got to the end, she turned around and retraced her steps, staring at the wall the whole way.

Once back to where she'd started, Mrs. Costello stopped. She cleared her throat.

I kept painting.

She cleared her throat again.

I still kept painting.

"You're a very good artist," she said.

I stopped painting.

My ears must have been playing tricks on me. That sounded just like a compliment, and Mrs. Costello was the last person I expected to get one of those from. There had to be a catch.

She looked up and down the wall. "What you've done here is beautiful. It looks so real." Then she turned back to me. "You are very talented."

I squinted up at her, waiting for the other shoe to drop.

Her forehead buckled into a frown. "So tell me why—why, if you can paint like this," she flung her arms toward the mural, "why on earth would you scribble dirty words like a five-year-old?" She shook her head. "I don't understand."

Then she started to walk away. She didn't even wait for an answer. She just said her bit and took off. It was like I wasn't there—like she'd been talking to herself.

And that made me mad. I dropped my paintbrush and jumped up.

"Do you want to?" I threw the question at her back.

She turned around.

"What?"

"Do you want to understand? You just

said you didn't know why I did the graffiti. Do you want me to tell you?"

Her body shifted backwards, like she was going to run.

"Look," I said, getting right to the point, "you asked a question. I'm asking you if you want an answer. Or do you even care what my reasons were?"

She had to have heard me—I was only two feet away from her. But she didn't say a word. She didn't even blink. She could have been a statue.

I shook my head. I was obviously wasting my breath.

"I didn't think so," I muttered and went back to work.

Chapter Ten

The next day was Saturday, and because I didn't work for Feniuk on the weekend, that meant I didn't have to get up early. I could lie in bed as long as I wanted.

It was the toilet flushing that woke me. Of course, as soon as my brain registered the sound, I drifted back to sleep, and the next time I surfaced, everything was quiet again. The thing that brought me back to consciousness permanently was the front door.

Slam! My body jerked and my eyes flew open. I squinted at the clock. It was 10:40. I had at least another good hour of sleep left in me.

Then the bedroom door burst open and the room started to vibrate. "Get up, you lazy slug," Dad boomed.

The words and volume were familiar, but the voice was way too cheerful. I cracked open an eye to make sure it was really my dad. I was still pretty groggy, but I could have sworn he was smiling.

I rolled over and put the pillow over my head. Dad pulled it away.

"Come on," he said again, jostling the bed with his knee. "Get up. I need you to help me."

"With what?" I mumbled into my mattress, making a last-ditch effort to hang onto sleep.

He ripped back the blankets. "With our new TV. I need you to help me carry it in."

Not only had Dad bought a new television, but a VCR too. As we carted them into the house, he informed me a satellite dish would be arriving on Wednesday.

My jaw just about hit the floor. I'd been trying to talk him into one of those for the last couple of years. "But –"

"I know what you're going to say," he cut me off. "But that was before, when we just had the old TV. It's different now. I mean, what's the point of having high-tech equipment if we can't get any channels? Right?"

He didn't wait for me to answer. Instead, he strode across the living room. "First thing we need to do is clear some space. Help me move this stuff out of the way."

Then he began dismantling Mom's music corner—chair, stand, sheet music, CDs, symphony programs—everything. For a year that corner had practically been a shrine, and now Dad was tearing it apart like a one-man wrecking crew.

At the risk of ruining his good mood, I said, "Are you sure you want to do that?"

He looked up. He wasn't smiling anymore. But when he spoke, he wasn't yelling either. His voice was quiet and matter-of-fact. "You said it yourself, son. She's not coming back."

It was true. I had said that. For a whole year I'd been telling myself she wasn't coming back. My mother had cut me out of her life, so I had cut her out of mine.

"But what if she does?" I heard myself reply.

It was weird how that turned out. Dad finally stopped pretending Mom wasn't gone, and I stopped acting like she'd never been there. So suddenly we weren't on opposite sides anymore. And that meant we didn't have to be mad at each other all the time. The situation hadn't really changed, but our way of looking at it had. And for some reason that seemed to make a difference.

It made a difference in other things too. Like the mural. When I checked it out on Monday, it didn't look the same. Don't get me wrong—nobody had messed with it. What was there looked just like it had on Friday. It was the stuff I hadn't painted that was causing the problem. Usually I don't have any trouble visualizing the things I'm going to draw. But that morning everything was a blur.

As I stood on the sidewalk trying to get my ideas to focus, Feniuk came around the corner of the building.

Walking toward me, he called, "So what's on the agenda today?"

Up to that point he'd let me do whatever I wanted, so his question surprised me. Maybe he'd guessed what I was planning. I eyed him warily. "Don't you trust me?"

He frowned. "It has nothing to do with trust. I'm just interested."

"I haven't decided yet," I hedged. Since I was having trouble visualizing images in my head, it was sort of the truth.

"Fair enough." He started back to the store. But then he stopped and turned around again. "Can I ask you something?"

What was it with adults? They were always asking questions.

"What?"

"When you're done here, how are we going to make sure you won't be buying anymore spray paint?"

I hadn't seen that one coming. So I didn't have an answer—at least not right away. My graffiti days were over, but I didn't want Feniuk to know that.

I shrugged. "Just don't sell it to me, I guess."

He shook his head. "You'd just get it somewhere else. I suppose what I'm really asking is what it's going to take to end the war between us."

This was unreal! The old man had zinged me again. I stared hard at him, trying to decide if he was serious. He looked like he was. I couldn't believe it. This was the chance I'd been waiting for. Finally somebody was willing to listen.

The only problem was that my thoughts were spinning so fast I couldn't sort them out. The guys and I had a lot of beefs. Where was I supposed to begin?

I must have been taking too long to decide, because suddenly Feniuk was talking again. "I know you and your friends think you've been treated unfairly, and in some ways you have."

"In *some* ways!" I went off like a firecracker. "How about in *every* way? You storekeepers have had it in for us from the very beginning. You never even gave us a chance. You just took one look at our clothes and hair and decided we were no good!"

Feniuk sighed. "I know it seems that way."

"It is that way!"

He shook his head. "No, it isn't. Not completely. I admit we kept an eye on you, but we were just being careful. The newspapers are filled with stories about women and seniors being attacked by teenagers. That's all we were thinking about. You may not realize it, but when you boys are together, you're a pretty intimidating group. The gang of you parked outside a store scares people away."

"But we never did anything," I argued. "We never hurt anybody. We don't do that kind of stuff."

"What about the broken window at Jackman's Market? Are you going to tell me you didn't do that?"

"That was an accident."

"So why did you run?"

I shook my head in disgust. "What choice did we have? We knew you wouldn't believe us. And you didn't, did you?"

He seemed to think about that for a while. Then he said, "What about the graffiti?"

"That was after," I grumbled.

"After what?"

"After you banned us from the shopping center. After you sicced the police on us. After we knew you were never going to listen."

Feniuk frowned. "Never's a long time. I'm listening now."

Chapter Eleven

The angrier Mike got, the faster he walked. The rest of us practically had to run to keep up.

"It's a crock!" He took his temper out on a stone. It ricocheted off a lamp standard and skittered onto the boulevard. Mike ignored it and kept walking. He hung a left at the corner.

"Why do you say that?" Danny called after him.

Mike didn't even bother to look back. "They're not going to change their minds."

"What makes you so sure?"

Mike spun around. "Have you forgotten? They hate us!"

"Maybe not," Horace said. "Maybe they're just afraid of us. If what Feniuk told Zee is true, Jackman and the others didn't intend this thing to snowball out of control any more than we did."

Mike's eyes widened. "Don't tell me you're on their side now too!"

I felt my back stiffen. Mike still thought I was a traitor for painting the mural.

I decided to turn the tables. "You act like you don't want this war to end."

He shot me a dirty look.

"Feniuk said he'd talk to the other merchants—explain our side," I pointed out for at least the fifth time. "He understands that we're not hanging around to cause trouble. Any stuff we've done was either an accident or self-defense. Feniuk is pretty sure he can make the other merchants see that."

I looked around at the group. Everyone seemed to be waiting for somebody else to do the talking.

As usual, it was Horace. He shrugged. "Okay—so we give it a few days. What have we got to lose?"

Horace had stuck his neck out for me with the other guys, but I don't know that he was any more convinced. It seemed like I was the only one who thought things were going to work out. Maybe it's because I'd been part of the negotiations. I'd been around Feniuk for nearly two weeks and I knew what he was like. Though the two of us might not see eye to eye on everything, I was pretty sure the old man would keep his word. But, of course, my friends couldn't know that. All they had to go by was me. And considering I was spending almost as much time with Feniuk as I was with them, I could understand why they were nervous.

I wished things would hurry up and get settled. I hated being stuck in the middle.

But after two days, nothing had changed. Well, actually there had been one change, but that had nothing to do with the guys and me. At least I don't think it did.

Bernie's Shoe Repair had gone out of business. Overnight the space had been cleared out and there was a For Lease sign in the window. Not a surprise really—if you think how many people wear runners these days. I might have thought my friends and I had scared him away, but none of us had ever even gone into that store. I guess nobody else had either.

As for the mural, it was finally starting to look like something, though not exactly what I'd planned. To one side of the door I'd painted a handful of merchants—Mrs. Costello, Bingham from the pharmacy, the guy who owned the hair salon, the Loonie Bin lady and, of course, Jackman. But instead of making them look mean and nasty and evil like I'd intended, I turned them into caricatures. They didn't totally look like themselves, but anyone who shopped at Fairhaven would recognize them and have a laugh.

Mike would've said I'd sold out, but I thought of the move more as insurance. I still wasn't finished the mural, and if things didn't work out, I'd go back to my original plan. But until the merchants made a decision about us, there was no sense getting them riled up.

Mrs. Costello was the first test. She showed up just as I was packing up for the day. The guy who owned the dry-cleaning store was with her.

"Ohhhhh!" she gasped, her gaze flitting over the entire mural and finally coming to rest on the caricature of herself.

Though I continued to pack up my stuff, I kept one eye on her. For about a minute, she didn't do anything but stare at the mural. I started to get worried. What if she hated it?

But I guess she didn't, because finally she put her hand over her mouth and started to giggle like a little girl. Then she pointed to the caricature and said to the guy from the dry cleaners, "Do you see that? It's me! It's a drawing of me."

The guy started to laugh. "Yeah. And it looks just like you. You and Peterson, Jackman, Mrs. Wilson and Bingham. You're all perfect. What a hoot!"

Mrs. Costello's smile evaporated and she wagged a finger under the guy's nose. "Didn't I tell you the boy was an artist?"

He nodded. "Yes, you did. You certainly did."

Though I was relieved that Mrs. Costello didn't mind seeing herself on the wall, it felt weird to hear myself being talked about like I wasn't there. I picked up my paint supplies and stood up to leave.

Instantly Mrs. Costello glommed onto my arm and pulled me toward the dry-cleaning guy as if she was showing off a prize poodle. "This is him," she beamed.

The guy stuck out his hand, and then realizing mine were full, he pulled it back again. "George Riley," he said. "I own Fairhaven Cleaners."

I nodded.

Mrs. Costello poked me in the back. "Well, tell him your name. Go on."

A couple of days ago the woman had been afraid to come near me, and now she was giving me etiquette lessons. I have no idea why I didn't tell her to mind her own business.

"Zee," I said to the guy.

"That's no kind of proper name," Mrs. Costello clucked her tongue in disgust.

I shrugged and turned to leave, but the guy stepped in front of Mrs. Costello and said, "Well, Zee, I have to tell you how impressed I am with your painting. For days now, Mrs. Costello has been bragging about you to anyone who'll listen. She thinks you must be related to Michelangelo. She says the only difference is that he worked on ceilings and you work on walls." He smiled self-consciously.

"Thanks," I mumbled and started for the store again.

"But I didn't come out here just to compliment you on your painting," Riley called after me.

I turned around. "No?"

He shook his head. "No. As I said, I really like your style. I can visualize something like what you've done here on the front window of my shop. I'd like to hire you to paint it—if you're interested," he added quickly.

Something inside me went ping—as if a wire that had been coiled tightly around my chest had suddenly been cut. I breathed deeply. I even allowed myself to smile.

"Thanks, Mr. Riley," I said. "That's cool. And I'd like to, except—"

Mrs. Costello pushed her way past the dry-cleaning guy. "Except what?" she demanded.

"Except I already have a job," I said, nodding toward the wall. "I work for Mr. Feniuk."

"Not anymore," said a voice behind me. It was Feniuk. Once again he'd sneaked up on me. He stuck a yellow receipt under my nose. There was a big red Paid in Full stamp on it.

Chapter Twelve

"I'm not that skinny," Benny protested. "And my nose isn't anywhere near that big."

"You wanna bet," Danny said. Of course, everybody laughed.

The guys were sprawled on the boulevard in front of the wall, watching me paint. Even though Feniuk had said my debt to him was paid, I had to finish the mural. It was a matter of pride. The old man had offered to pay me, but I couldn't let him do that. After all, I was the one who'd messed up the wall in the first place. Anyway, as soon as I was done, I'd be painting the window at Fairhaven Cleaners. And I would be getting paid for that.

I moved on to the caricature of Mike. I curled his lip like Elvis, and around his neck I put a wide leather band with metal spikes.

"He looks like a bulldog!" Benny howled, obviously glad it was someone else's turn to be in the hot seat.

Doing his best to look like the painting, Mike waved his studded wristband in Benny's face. "And don't you forget it," he snarled.

It was great to see everybody in a good mood again. We still hadn't found out if we were welcome in the shopping center, but Feniuk, Riley and Mrs. Costello were clearly on our side, and that was a start.

"Why so many chains?" Horace complained when I got around to painting him.

"I know you said a caricature is supposed to exaggerate stuff, but there's so much metal around my neck it's a wonder I can stand up. And what's with the head? Do you think it could get any bigger?"

"That's a question we all ask," I grinned.

Horace opened his mouth to zing me back, but a woman's scream cut him off.

I guess we should've stayed out of it, but there was so much commotion going on outside Jackman's Market, we had to find out what it was about. Besides, by the time we got there, a huge crowd had gathered and no one noticed us anyway.

A woman was sobbing and clawing at Jackman's chest. "My daughter, Jessica, I only took my eyes off her for a second! Where could she have gone?"

"She can't be far." Jackman patted the woman's back in an effort to comfort her. But she just wailed louder.

"What happened?" I whispered to a woman in the crowd.

She shook her head. "The lady's little girl wandered off."

That's when we heard the police sirens.

"C'mon." Horace instantly started jogging toward the street. I thought he just wanted to clear off before the cops arrived, but when we hit the sidewalk, he said, "Okay, Mike, you and Benny take Beaverbrook. Go a couple of blocks if you have to. Zee, you and Danny look on Madison. I'm gonna search Fontaine. How far can a little kid get in five minutes? One of us is bound to see her."

He was right. Danny and I hadn't even gone a block when we heard Horace whistle. By the time we caught up with him he was halfway across the shopping center parking lot, heading for Jackman's Market. And there was a little girl riding on his shoulders.

"Hello," she beamed at us. She had one of Horace's chains around her neck, and it was puddling on the top of Horace's head.

"Jessica!" The little girl's mother came running toward us at full speed.

"Hi, Mommy," Jessica smiled.

Horace put the little girl down. Instantly the woman swallowed her up in her arms. Eventually, of course, Jessica started to squirm, and the lady had no choice but to let her loose. Hanging onto the kid with one hand, the woman stood up and put out her other hand to Horace.

"Thank you," she said, and you could tell she meant it. "Thank you so much."

The crowd—which had followed the woman over—broke into applause.

Horace grinned self-consciously. "You're welcome, but I didn't really do anything. She was playing with a cat in somebody's yard. I just called her name and she came." Then his expression got all serious again and he said, "But you know, lady, you really ought to teach your little girl not to go with strangers. What if I'd been a weirdo or somethin'?"

Even the guys and I could see what a goofy thing that was to say, and we laughed right along with everyone else.

Until Jackman stepped up.

The day got quiet again, and I held my breath. Jackman stuck his hand out. For a few seconds Horace just looked at it. Finally he took it—and shook it—Jackman with it. The crowd laughed again. So did Jackman and Horace.

And that's when I knew everything was going to be okay.

I waited until everyone had cleared off the shopping center parking lot before I headed back to the wall. There was still one more part to do on the mural, and I wanted to do it alone.

When I was done, I stood on the boulevard and drank it in. I thought about how I'd tried to send a message to the merchants with my graffiti—and how that had failed. Then I thought about Horace and Jackman shaking hands. I looked at the mural again. Yeah. It was right. It told the story as it really was.

It was a storefront. There was a door in the middle and display windows on both sides.

A blue-and-yellow awning hung overhead. On one side of the door stood the merchants, eying the broken window in the door and the incriminating soccer ball on the sidewalk. On the other side of the door stood the guys—the obvious culprits. And in the middle, kneeling on the sidewalk and picking up the pieces of glass, were Feniuk and me.

"I told you that door needed something, didn't I?" Feniuk said from behind me. "You were bound to figure it out sooner or later."

I turned. Feniuk was smiling, but for once it didn't bug me. Jackman was standing beside him. And surprisingly, that didn't bug me either.

Jackman was soaking up the mural and moving his head up and down like one of those bobble-head dolls.

"It's good," he said.

"Thanks," I replied and began gathering up my paint things for the last time.

They watched me for a while, and then Jackman cleared his throat. "You know," he said, "one of the problems with getting old is that you forget that you used to be young."

I thought about that. Since I hadn't been old yet, I couldn't really argue. So I nodded.

I hadn't realized Jackman had been holding his breath until he let it out in a gush. "Did you see the shoe repair shop has closed?" he asked.

"Yeah," I said. "I saw that."

"It's a small space—hard to rent." He cleared his throat again. "Well, the thing is, the other merchants and I have been talking, and we thought that...I mean there's no point in having the place sit empty...we can't have you kids standing around the—"

"Leo," Feniuk interrupted, "if you don't get to the point soon, the boy will be as old as we are."

Jackman frowned and waved him away. "All right, all right." Then he looked back at me. "It's like this. You kids need a place.

We have one. I can't promise you it'll be forever, but until something better comes along…" He shrugged. "Well, it's a start. What do you say? If you're willing to give it a shot, so are we."

NEW
Orca Soundings novel

Overdrive by Eric Walters

"Go! Get out of here!"

I saw flashing red lights behind me in the distance. For a split second I took my foot off the accelerator. Then I pressed down harder and took a quick left turn.

Jake has finally got his driver's license, and tonight he has his brother's car as well. He and his friend Mickey take the car out and cruise the strip. When they challenge another driver to a road race, a disastrous chain reaction causes an accident. Jake and Mickey leave the scene, trying to convince themselves they were not involved. The driver of the other car was Luke, a one-time friend of Jakes. Jake finds he cannot pretend it didn't happen and struggles with the right thing to do. Should he pretend he was not involved and hope Luke doesn't remember? Or should he go to the police?

Blue Moon by Marilyn Halvorson

Bobbie Jo didn't set out to buy a limping blue roan mare—she wanted a colt she could train to barrel race. But the horse is a fighter, just like Bobbie Jo, and that's what made up her mind. Now all she has to do is train the sour old mare that obviously has a past. While she nurses the horse back to health and they get to know each other, Bobbie Jo realizes that the mare, now called Blue Moon, may have more history than she first thought. With the help of the enigmatic Cole McCall, she slowly turns the horse into a barrel racer. Then, when everything seems to be going well, she finds out the truth about Blue Moon and where she came from. Will Bobbie Jo be able to keep the horse? And will she find out why Cole seems to have so many secrets?

NEW
Orca Soundings novel

Thunderbowl by Lesley Choyce

Jeremy's band is hot—really hot. Thunderbowl is on the way up, and they have had their first big break. After beating archrivals The Mongrel Dogs in a Battle of the Bands they have landed a long-term gig at a local bar, and now a record company might be interested. The only problem is that when Jeremy should be doing his homework and keeping up in school, he is spending most nights in a rowdy club, trying to keep the band together while his life is falling apart and he is pretending to be older than he actually is. Trying to balance his dreams of success with the hard realities of the music business, Jeremy is forced to make some hard choices.

Other titles in the
ORCA SOUNDINGS series.